WOMEN at Their Work

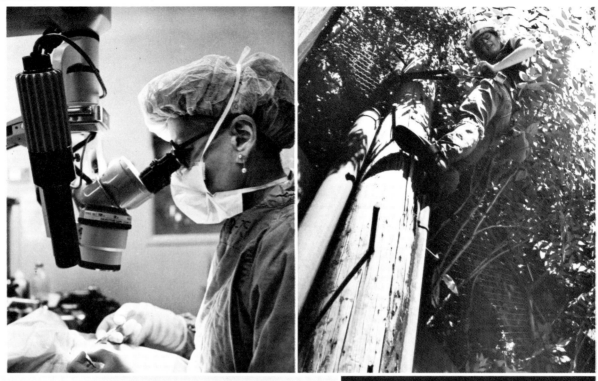

WOMEN at Their Work
by Betty Lou English

Dial Books for Young Readers

New York

Published by Dial Books for Young Readers
A Division of NAL Penguin Inc.
2 Park Avenue
New York, New York 10016
Published simultaneously in Canada
by Fitzhenry & Whiteside Limited, Toronto

Library of Congress Catalog Card Number: 76-42924
Printed in the U.S.A.
First Pied Piper Printing 1988
C O B E
10 9 8 7 6 5 4 3 2 1

A Pied Piper Book is a registered trademark of
Dial Books for Young Readers,
a division of NAL Penguin Inc.,
® TM 1,163,686 and ® TM 1,054,312.

WOMEN AT THEIR WORK
is published in a hardcover edition by
Dial Books for Young Readers.
ISBN 0-8037-0496-8

For Pat

Preparing
cake decorations

Arranging
hors d'oeuvres

Preparing
sea bass entree

Chef

Ever since I was a child, I have loved to cook. As I grew older, it became my hobby. So I decided that I should make my living at what I liked to do most.

My job is to prepare fish and sauces for several of the restaurants in a large hotel. I have to get to the kitchen early in the morning and start right away to cook the sauces—twenty gallons for just one day. Soon it is time to serve lunch. I continue to stir the sauces so they won't burn while I prepare the lunch orders the waiters bring in. Today we are serving shrimp, scallops, and sea bass. In the afternoon I prepare food for the evening and the next day. My day ends at 3 o'clock, when another chef takes over for the evening.

When I first came to the hotel, I was a pastry cook. Then I worked for a time making and decorating fancy foods for parties and banquets. I learned all of these jobs by reading and watching, but mostly by trying things out myself. Some day I hope to be Executive Chef of a small restaurant where I can try out new ways to make delicious food. My husband is also a chef, and right now we're writing a cookbook together.

*Conferring in chambers
with a defense attorney*

Judge

Everyone should be treated fairly. That's what I believe. And that's why I wanted to be a judge—to prove it could be done. I'm proud that I was a lawyer for many years before becoming a criminal court judge. I really learned the law.

The youngest of my three children calls my robe "that black nightgown." The custom of judges wearing robes began in England. Law students wore a black gown, then later as judges they added a white collar, black tie, and wig. I don't think the robe is needed, though, to show authority. In my court I insist that everyone speak quietly and treat each other with respect.

I love to listen to really fine lawyers argue their cases. It is a beautiful thing when a lawyer does this well. I am always talking about the law with lawyers, and I like to meet with them before a case begins to be sure they understand the law involved. This helps to prevent unnecessary trials.

The best part of being a judge is seeing people who have been in trouble leave my court and do well. Recently I received a letter from a prisoner I had sentenced. He thanked me for some advice I had given him and told me that he's going to college in prison and making plans for his future. That really made me feel good.

With Short George,
a "common" (mean) horse

On the practice
track at Belmont
(below right)

Jockey

When I was a little girl growing up in Iowa, I loved to visit my grandparents' farm. Every holiday my grandfather would give me a new animal: sheep, goats, geese, ducks—everything.

After I was grown up, my husband took me to the races one day, and I thought, "That looks like fun." But I couldn't become a jockey right away. First I got a job as an exercise girl, walking the horses. After a year I started training to be a jockey.

I get up at 4:30 A.M. so I can be at the track by 6:00. In the morning I ride six or seven horses on the practice track. Sometimes we take a slow canter, sometimes an easy gallop. But what I like best is "breezing." That's when the horse takes hold of the bit and I just lean back and we go very fast.

After I take the last horse back to the barn, I have to clean the tack—the saddle, bridle, and girth. Then, not every afternoon, but many afternoons, I ride in the races. When I get home in the evenings, I'm very tired and go to bed early.

The hardest thing about being a jockey is getting up at 4:30 every morning. You really have to love riding to do that. And the most exciting thing is winning a race.

Reading from the
Torah at the pulpit

Holding the Torah
in its mantle

Rabbi

When I was a child, I thought I would be a teacher when I grew up. Then I decided I wanted to teach religion. So I became a rabbi. I am the first woman in this country ever to become a rabbi.

To prepare myself for my work I went to college for four years and then to rabbinical school for four more years. I also served as a student rabbi. Now I have my own congregation.

Every day is different for me. I conduct worship services on the Sabbath. On other days I teach Hebrew, lead study groups, counsel people with problems, visit the sick in the hospital, work with children in our nursery school, attend many different kinds of meetings, conduct weddings and funerals, and travel around the country telling people what it is like to be the first woman rabbi.

The part of my job that is most exciting to me is preaching and conducting worship services. The hardest part is answering all my mail. And what I like most about it is helping people.

Welding

Casting in the foundry

Sculptor

My life is spent in my studio. This is where I do my thinking and dreaming. This is where a sculpture begins and where I finally see the finished work of art.

Most of my sculptures are done in bronze. I start with an idea, something I want to say with my art. Usually this idea has a shape. First I make a model in clay. Sometimes it changes as I work on it and get new ideas. When I am happy with the clay design, the next step is to make a mold in exactly the same shape. Into this mold I will pour the liquid bronze. It is very hot—ten times hotter than boiling water —so I have to wear special clothing to protect myself from burns: leather chaps to protect my legs and a leather apron over the upper part of my body. I remember the first time I poured bronze for a sculpture—it was very early on a fall morning, and the rising sun and the bronze filled the room with light. It was beautiful.

When the sculpture is finished and I can see the result of my idea in front of me—that is the most exciting moment for an artist.

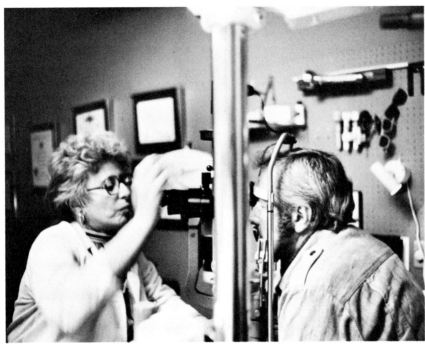

Examining a patient

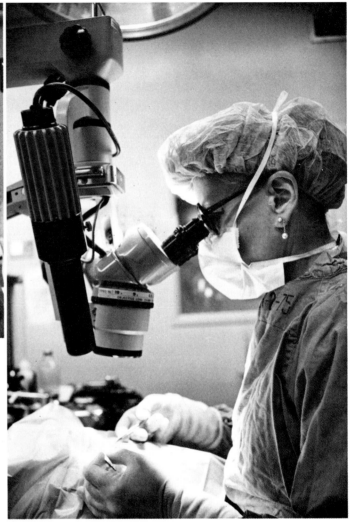

In the operating room,
using the operating microscope

Ophthalmologist

One of the things I love about my work is that every day is different. Some mornings I am in the operating room performing eye surgery. In the afternoons I see patients in my office. One morning a week I teach, and on Saturdays I visit my patients in the hospital. Doing research and going to medical meetings—those are important things, too.

I was in high school when I decided to become a doctor. But it wasn't until I was in medical school that I decided to be an ophthalmologist. I liked surgery so much. I also saw that I could do full justice to this very important work, and still arrange my hours so that I could spend time with my family. I have four children who are grown-up now, and one of them, my daughter Ellen, is an ophthalmologist too.

Surgery is the most exciting part of my work. You have only a short time to do a difficult job that is so important. You must decide when to operate and when not to, and you must get the patient ready for the operation. But it is all worthwhile when you test a patient after an operation and he or she can see again. After the bandages are taken off I have heard a patient say, "Doctor, you're so beautiful!" Who wouldn't like to hear that?

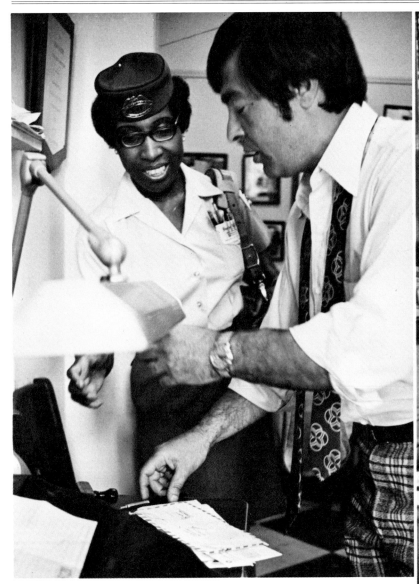

Delivering mail

*Leaving the post office
to begin her rounds*

Letter Carrier

As a little girl I wanted to be a truck driver when I grew up. The day I saw a woman dressed in a letter carrier's uniform driving a postal truck was the day I decided to become a letter carrier.

My working day begins at 6 A.M. when I arrive at the post office to begin getting the mail ready. Because I work on a business route—delivering mail to office buildings—I make three deliveries a day. At 7:30 I leave the post office for my first delivery. Two hours later I am back at the post office to begin again. My other two deliveries are at 10:30 A.M. and at 1:00 P.M. My workday ends at about 2:30 P.M., and I can head for home.

The hardest part of my job is when someone I work with is sick and I have to do the work of two people and still make my deliveries on time. The most exciting part is when I deliver a check for a large sum of money. Seeing how happy this makes people makes me happy too.

Nailing a corner board

Sawing a board that will
be used to repair a cottage

Carpenter

I grew up in Ohio. One day I received a postcard from a friend who was vacationing on Martha's Vineyard. It was a picture of one of the island beaches, and I said, "That's where I want to be."

So I came here and got a job as a waitress, but that was just for the summer. The next summer I came back and got housepainting and carpentry jobs. And now I live here all year round. I think if you really believe in yourself and in what you want to do, you can do it.

Most of my work is on houses: putting in windows, laying floors, building shelves, fixing roofs, putting on shingles, finishing porches. A while ago I worked on a film crew, helping to build sets. We constructed a boardwalk, beach cabanas, a gazebo, houses, and a mock-up of a boat.

I have always liked to do carpentry. When I was little, my father gave me my own tools and workbench. I learned a lot by watching other people do a job and then doing it myself. A job like shingling where you do the same thing over and over again isn't very interesting. But finishing something and having it look nice —that's the part I like best.

Checking negatives in the darkroom
and preparing to use the enlarger

Photographer

I decided to become a photographer because I always enjoyed taking pictures, and it was something I did well. I learned about photography from attending courses and workshops. But a lot of what I know comes from experience.

On a day when I am photographing a story, I first check my equipment to make sure it is in working order, that my cameras are loaded, and that I have enough of the right kind of film for the job. After I finish photographing, I take my films to the laboratory that develops them. While I am there, I often pick up work that was left earlier. I look at the results and order the prints I will need. My day also usually includes phone calls to companies and magazines to try to line up new jobs. At night or on weekends I sometimes work in my home darkroom on photographs that are special to me.

Photography is hard work. The most difficult part is selling the photographs and finding new work. But even that is fun. I enjoy meeting new people and getting to know their lives a little bit. And of course the best part of all is taking a fine photograph.

Teaching medical students about Puerto Rican customs, and (below right) sharing a Puerto Rican meal

A student examines a Puerto Rican baby, using her training in medical-Spanish to communicate with the baby's mother.

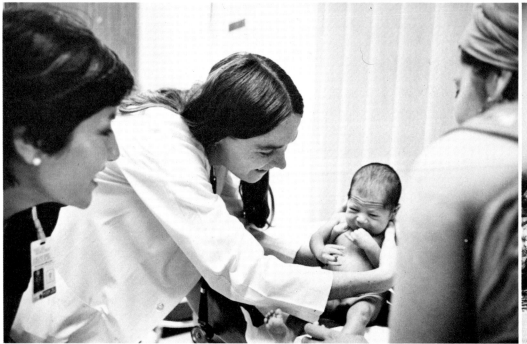

Medical-Spanish Program Director

When I was a little girl, I went to a hospital clinic with my mother. She spoke only Spanish, and the doctors spoke only English. I helped them understand each other, but I was unhappy that the doctors couldn't speak my mother's language.

After I was grown up, I met a man who had written a book teaching doctors how to speak Spanish to their Puerto Rican patients. He wanted someone to use his book in a special program at a medical school in New York City, where there are many Spanish-speaking people. I decided to try.

We teach medical students how to ask a patient about his illness and to understand the patient's reply. We teach about Puerto Rican customs, too. We go to a Puerto Rican market to buy food, then take it home and cook it. In the summer some students visit Puerto Rico to learn more. Understanding the language and the way people live makes a doctor better able to help patients when they are sick.

Last year I had a student who didn't seem to be enjoying the course. But then I saw her a few months later, at Christmas. She told me she was working with children and had been able to speak Spanish to a little Puerto Rican boy. She was so happy, she kissed me. And I thought, "This is my Christmas present."

Telephone Installer

When I was a little girl, I wanted to be an astronaut. Later I found that I loved being outdoors and working with my hands. As a telephone installer I am outside a lot, and I'm also on my own. I like that.

My day begins at 8 A.M., when I receive my work orders. These tell me where I will be installing telephones that day. Then I pick up the telephones that will be needed, and they are loaded on my truck. After this I am off to my calls.

Before I could become an installer, I had to go to school for six weeks. While I was learning pole-climbing, I fell off and hurt my leg. But I was determined to get over my fear of heights. So as soon as my leg was better, I went back to school. Now I'm a pretty good pole climber.

A funny thing happened once when I was installing a telephone in the basement of a house. The family had such a good watchdog that he wouldn't let me upstairs when I was finished. I called to the woman, but she didn't hear me. So finally I called her on the phone I had just installed. She took the dog away. And I got out of the basement.

At the head of the
foreign news desk

Watching the delivery
trucks pull out

Newspaper Editor

When I was little, I wanted to be a movie star, then a ballet dancer, then a poet, then a writer of any kind. In seventh grade I worked for my first school newspaper, and that's when I decided on the newspaper business. One other thing I wanted was to live in New York and to be in the center of things. Now I work for *The New York Times*. Times Square is the center of New York, *The Times* is the center of Times Square, and I am almost in the middle of *The Times*.

I am a copy editor for the foreign news. I check the articles written by reporters before they are printed in the paper. The names and facts must be right, everything has to be spelled properly, the sentences must be easy to understand, and the story must be the right length. The copy editors also write the headlines to tell in a few words what a long story is about.

Working on school newspapers helped me to learn my job, and so did hanging around print shops asking to try things. I also went to college, and then I studied journalism in graduate school. Learning to do something well and then improving on that skill is one of the greatest things in the world.

The hardest part of an editor's job is having to sit at a desk for most of the working day. The most exciting part is knowing that something you do well will reach so many people. When we write a good headline or explain a complicated idea, more than 800,000 people will see our work and learn from it. The President of the United States will read it, and so will children in school.

Working with the cast of Kismet *in a dress rehearsal for a performance at Wolf Trap*

Conducting the orchestra

Orchestra Conductor

I always wanted to be a musician. My parents loved music, and I learned to play the piano when I was very young. Later I studied at the Juilliard School of Music in New York.

After graduation I continued with the piano, and soon I was hired to play for a ballet company that was going to tour Europe. When we got on the plane, the director asked me if I had ever done any conducting. When I said yes, he handed me all of the music. At the last minute the conductor had been unable to come, so I was it!

When we are preparing a musical show, my days are very busy. I may have a three-hour orchestra rehearsal in the morning. In the afternoon I'll meet with the singers to help them with their parts. Then in the evening, from six to eleven, we'll rehearse the whole show. I enjoy working with people, helping them to express the music as the composer wrote it. This is the most exciting part of being a conductor.

Besides conducting, I also write music, and have composed and performed my own piano concerto. I still love to play the piano. I'm so lucky—doing all three things I enjoy most.

*In uniform with
fire engine and
helping to extinguish
a brush fire*

Firefighter

Our town has 100 volunteer firefighters, and I am proud to be one of them. Since I'm on fire call 24 hours a day, I have a Home Unit—it's like a radio—to receive the fire calls. A code tells what kind of fire it is: a brush fire or a car fire or a house fire. Most fires happen between noon and 6 P.M.

When a call comes, I go to the firehouse, put on my boots, coat, and helmet, climb on the fire engine, and hurry to the fire. Sometimes I drive the engine. When we get to the fire, a search team is sent in to see exactly where it is located and if there are any people in danger. Putting out a fire usually takes about an hour and a half. When we get back to the firehouse, we clean all the equipment and put it away so it's ready for the next call.

Before I could become a firefighter, I had to take a year and a half of training Our department also meets once a month to practice all the things we need to do to put out a fire—ladder climbing, hose handling, and using tools like the crowbar and pike. For me the hardest job is packing and unpacking the hose on the fire engine.

Every year each fire department in our county chooses its Firefighter of the Year. Last year, when the awards were announced, I was so surprised to hear my name. It was the second most exciting thing that has happened to me in my whole life. The most exciting happened more recently—I've just been hired as a professional firefighter.

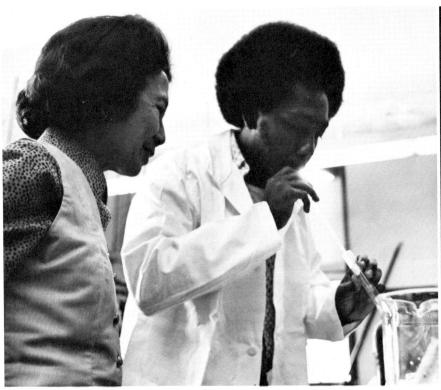

With a student

Working in the
chemistry lab

Chemist

In the Philippines where I grew up, going to school is considered very important. My father wanted me to go to college, and since our family had a drugstore, it seemed natural to me to study pharmacy. From there I went on to chemistry, and studied for my advanced degree at the University of Michigan. Now I am a college professor and chairman of the Chemistry Department.

In the mornings I teach a three-hour class, and most of that time is spent in the lab. Sometimes being a chemist is like being a detective. When I work in the lab with my students, I teach them how to figure out what's in an unknown substance. It's like solving a mystery.

During the rest of the day I am busy with my work as head of the Chemistry Department. This includes buying equipment for the laboratory, helping students who have problems, and attending meetings with other teachers. In the summer I spend part of my time working on research projects.

The hardest part of my job is having to give a student a failing grade. Seeing my students getting ahead in their studies is the nicest part. Some go on to graduate school or medical school. It makes me happy to see them using what they learned here and doing well.

*At the wheel of
a radio car*

*Taking information
about a bicycle theft*

Police Officer

My father was a railroad policeman, and I have cousins who are policemen. When I was about thirteen, I saw a television program about a policewoman, and that's when I decided that I would be one too.

I work on eight-hour shifts, some days from 8 A.M. to 4 P.M., some from 4 P.M. to midnight, and others from midnight to 8 A.M. I am assigned to one section of town, and I patrol that area in a police car. When I hear a call on the police radio that begins, "Car six respond to . . . " I answer, "Ten-four," which means, "Okay, I've got the call."

Today I received a call to help a boy who had hurt his leg playing in the woods. I helped get him to the hospital. After that I talked to a man whose son's bicycle had been stolen. I wrote down all the information so we can try to get the bicycle back for him. Some of the other things I do include checking the houses of people who are away on vacation, making sure no cars are parked where they shouldn't be, and stopping drivers who are speeding or breaking other traffic laws.

One time I had a call to help a woman who had been bitten by a huge dog. I got the woman into the police car, but then the dog kept coming after me. So I got on the car radio and called for help. I said, "Send additional units. This dog is as big as a pony!" This was picked up by a special radio station that broadcasts interesting police calls, and pretty soon my mixed-up message was heard all over the world.

On the air with guests Susan and Martin Tolchin

Radio Interviewer

People like to be interviewed. I get about a hundred requests a week from people who want to be on my show. I choose a person who has recently been in the news or the author of a new book or someone who is doing something that I think listeners will be interested in hearing about.

After I decide whom I want to interview, I call the person to arrange a date. This is called the "booking." My guest and I get to the studio fifteen minutes before the show. Sitting at a table with microphones in front of us, we face the control booth where the engineer is. He signals us when to begin and when to stop. The program is a half-hour long, and the time goes very quickly.

I decided that I wanted to be an interviewer after having been interviewed myself on a radio show. This person did it so well, letting me say what I wanted to say, that I decided I wanted to give other people that same kind of chance. And now I have had my own show for three years.

Most of the people I choose to interview are women, and it's very exciting for me to give them the chance to tell people about what they've done. One of the nicest parts of my job is getting mail from listeners who like the program. My husband and three children always have comments about my programs too, sometimes good, and sometimes not so good.

*A ceramic and feather
wall hanging by Yeffe Kimball*

*Thinking about an
unfinished painting*

Painter, Sculptor, Writer, and Illustrator

I was born in an earth lodge in Oklahoma. An earth lodge is a dugout in the ground. My father was an Osage Indian, my mother, a white woman from a pioneer family. Part of my childhood was spent on a ranch in Missouri. I milked the cows, fed the chickens, and had my own horse. Since I was only seven when I was given my horse, I was too small to mount it from the ground, so they built me a little stoop to climb up on.

I always knew that I wanted to be an artist. I started painting when I was four or five years old. Later I studied at the Art Students League in New York City and in Paris and Italy. Now I have a studio in my home, where I paint almost every day of my life. I like to do huge paintings, so it takes many weeks to finish one. It makes me happy and proud that people like my paintings. They have been exhibited all over the world, and I have had eighty one-woman shows.

Besides my painting, I also do illustrations for books and have written and researched a number of books about the American Indian, many of them for children. Now I am working on a very exciting project: collecting Native American painting, sculpture, ceramics, and mixed media for a national exhibition. It is very important to me that people know about Indian history and culture. I feel it is the only real heritage this country has. It is especially important for Indian children to know the history of their people. And other children should learn the true Indian history and way of life; the reverence for nature and all living and growing things that mother earth provides.

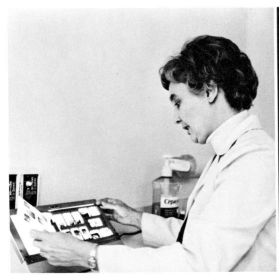

Viewing x-rays

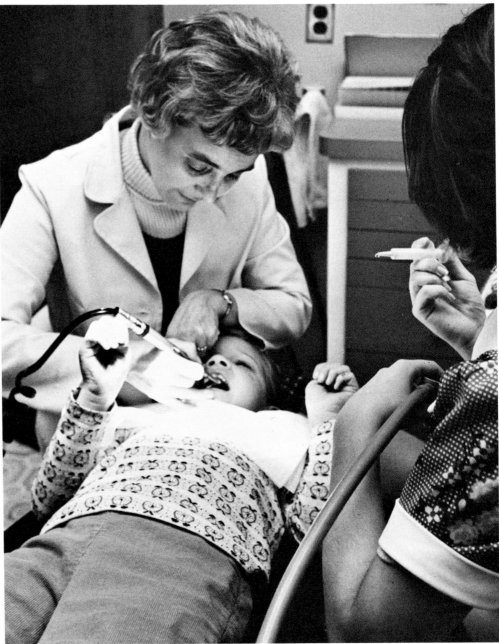

Cleaning a patient's teeth

Dentist

I am a pediatric dentist—a dentist who takes care of children's teeth. When I was a little girl, I wanted to become a doctor, and a dentist is one type of doctor. I decided to become a children's dentist because I enjoy working with my hands and I like children and want to help them. I am married and have four children of my own, so I'm glad I can arrange my days and hours in the office according to the needs of my family. This is easy to do as a dentist.

Some days I see patients in the office and other days I travel to the city to teach dentistry at the university.

At the office, when a child comes in to see me, I explain what we are going to do that day. This may be checking the teeth or cleaning them, or whatever else is needed—perhaps taking x-rays or giving a fluoride treatment to make the teeth strong.

When we are finished, the patient chooses a prize from our treasure chest. At this time I talk with the parents to explain what we did and what the treatment may be at the next appointment. After the visit is over, I write down all that was done on the patient's card. Then I am ready to see the next patient.

At the university I teach young people who are studying to be dentists. I show them ways to treat people's teeth, and I watch the students as they treat their own patients.

There are many parts of my job that I like. One of the nicest is seeing a patient who at first didn't want to visit the dentist come back again with a smile.

*Heading back to the dock
after taking a family
to their boat (below)*

Launch Operator

My job is to take people to and from their boats, which are moored in the harbor. I also assign boats to moorings, check to see that boats are at the correct moorings, and collect mooring and launch fees. Some weeks I work during the day, and some weeks I work at night. Working at night in the darkness isn't so hard—unless it gets foggy. Then I have to go slowly and carefully, using my compass.

The hardest part of handling the launch is making a good landing, coming alongside a boat or the dock without bumping. Once one of my passengers said I drive better than the men. I asked her what she meant. "You don't crash into the boats," she said. But I don't really think the men do, either.

I always knew I wanted to work outdoors and away from the city. I love the water, and I love boats. My father always had a boat, and he taught me all about sailing. Now I live on a very old and very beautiful 70-foot coasting schooner.

Checking a weather report

In the cockpit

Airline Pilot

My father's hobby was piloting small planes, and that is how I got interested in flying. I was so frightened during my first lesson that I got sick to my stomach, but I kept on learning to fly, and later I taught two of my brothers how to fly. By the time I applied for my job as copilot, I had flown nearly 4,000 hours.

I fly about sixteen days each month, sometimes for as long as twelve hours a day. There's a lot to do before flight time. That's why I have to get to the airport an hour before we take off. First, before going on the plane, I make out the flight plan. Then, half an hour before take-off, I check all the equipment inside the plane: instruments, radios, emergency exits. The captain flies the first leg of the trip—from one airport to another—I fly the next, and so on. While the captain is flying I do all the radio work. Our airline makes a lot of short flights, which means a lot of take-offs and landings. I have done as many as seventeen landings in one day.

People think that take-offs and landings are the hardest part of flying. But really it is coping with bad weather: thunderstorms, ice, flying in clouds. For me, the most exciting part is going into an airport I've never been to before. And just the flying part. I really love to fly.

Our airline has five hundred pilots, and I'm the only woman. When I wrote for an application I used my initial rather than my name. The application came addressed to Mr. B. Wiley. But except for one man who doesn't like the idea of a woman being a pilot, everyone treats me as just another pilot doing my job.

WOMEN AT THEIR WORK is Betty Lou English's first book and grew out of her desire to show women involved in and caring about their work, individuals whose sense of life as a whole has been heightened by realizing their professional ambitions. Represented here are women from all walks of life: single and married; young and old; Black, white, Puerto Rican, Native American, and Filipino; professionals, technicians, and skilled workers; sportswomen and artists. Each woman has been interviewed at length, and great care has been taken to insure that the words that appear in this book reflect each one's individuality and personality.

Says Betty Lou English of her own work: "Being a photographer is one of the most exhilarating and gratifying jobs in the world. I love meeting so many different kinds of people. Photographing them and talking with them, I get to know how they feel about things that are important to all of us. And each time some of that shows in the photograph, I feel a wish has come true."